A message from the author,

Just like people, dogs come in all different shapes, sizes, and colors. There are blind dogs, deaf dogs, and some even use wheelchairs. The thing to remember is that they all have value. Blind dogs can live happy and fun lives with loving families. Just like Digger.

Thank you, I hope you enjoy our story.

Always supervise children in the company of animals.
Do not allow your dog to ingest foreign objects.

First Printing, 2017

ISBN-13: 978-1548068738
ISBN-10: 154806873X

Watching out for Digger

Written by
Cathy Symons

Illustrated by
Anne Zimanski

It is an exciting day for Patrick and Hannah. They have waited a long time for this day to come.

Today, they are going to the shelter to adopt a dog.

They have dreamed about all the fun things they will get to do with their new dog,

like running,

jumping,

and playing.

Their mom brings them to the pet store to get all the things their new dog will need.

They pick out a bed, a bowl, food, and plenty of toys.

Then they are off to the shelter.

When they arrive, the shelter worker greets them and asks,

"What kind of dog are you looking for?"

"We have big dogs, small dogs, dogs with lots of hair and some with no hair at all."

"We want a dog that likes to go for walks, and is always looking to play and have fun!" Patrick says.

"Great! We have just the dog for you."

"Meet Digger"

"But the sign says he is blind. How can he do the fun things that we want him to do?" Patrick asks.

The shelter worker explains that blind dogs can have fun too. They can learn tricks, go for walks and play. Just like every other dog.

"Having a dog is a lot of work but having a blind dog takes a little more responsibility."

The shelter worker also explains that since Digger cannot see, both Patrick and Hannah will need to follow some rules in order to keep Digger safe.

Here is a list of safety rules

1. Put all of your toys away so that Digger won't trip over them
2. Block the stairs so that Digger does not fall down them
3. Watch out for Digger and be sure that he does not bump his head
4. Keep the door leading outside locked so Digger does not go outside by himself

When Patrick and Hannah get home, they pick up all of their toys and block the stairs with a baby gate.

Patrick and Hannah spend the day coming up with ideas to keep Digger safe.

They crawl around on the floor at Digger's level to see what he can bump into and decide to wrap all the chairs and table legs in bubble wrap.

They cut up pool noodles and put them around the fireplace. Their mom puts new latches on the doors to make sure they stay fully closed.

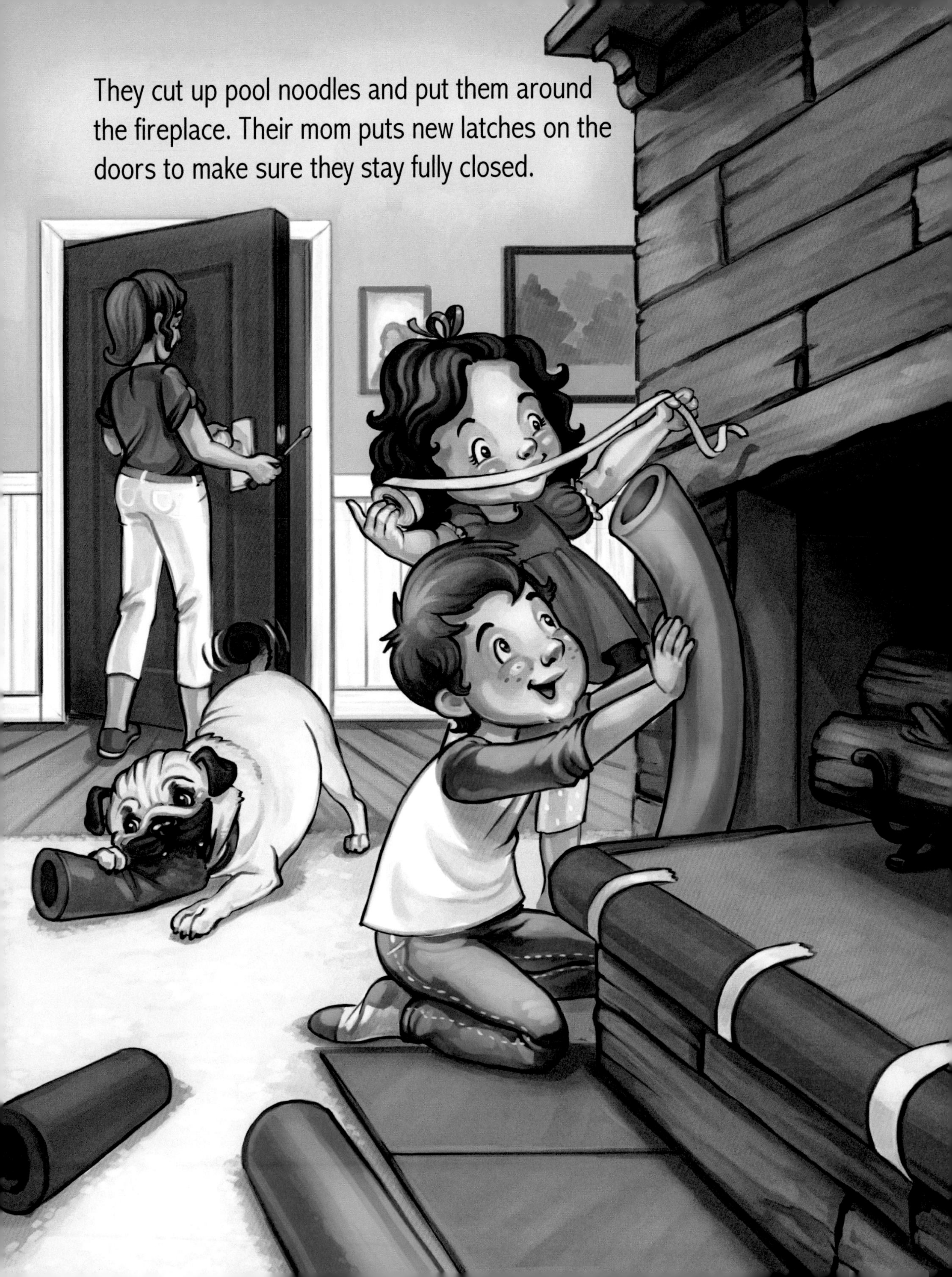

She also posts the list of safety rules on the refrigerator so that everyone can see them.

Patrick and Hannah are happy with all they have done to keep Digger safe in the house.

However, they wonder how they will keep him safe outside.

"I know what we can do! We can use pillows to keep him safe, kind of like making a pillow sandwich," Patrick exclaims as he places a pillow on each side of Digger.

Hannah laughs as Digger rolls over onto his back like a turtle.

"We could try using a helmet," says Hannah. "It always keeps me safe when I am riding my bike, so maybe it will work for Digger too."

She goes to the garage and comes back with a pink and purple bike helmet. She places it on Digger's head but it is too big and ends up sliding forward onto his snout.

"How about we fill the yard with balloons," Patrick says as he jumps up and down with excitement. "That should keep him safe. If he runs into them he will bounce right off!"

They try blowing up balloons but Digger keeps running through them and they float away.

"Let's try using bubbles!" Hannah yells as she blows bubbles everywhere.

They float around the yard only for a few moments before landing and popping.

"I know. We can make him a suit of marshmallows," Patrick shouts as he opens a new bag of fresh marshmallows, but Digger quickly eats them.

Hannah scratches her head for a moment. “I have a great idea, follow me.”

She runs inside to the closet and digs out her old Halloween costumes.

"I was a Triceratops for Halloween last year," she says as she finds the costume and puts it on Digger.

"The horns will keep him from bumping his head."

Patrick, Hannah and Digger play in the yard all afternoon, pretending to be dinosaurs.

When Digger finally falls asleep, he is happy and safe. Dreaming of marshmallows.

The End

About the Author

Cathy Symons is a veterinary technician and has spent 25 years caring for animals. She is the author of "*Blind Devotion Enhancing the Lives of Blind and Visually Impaired Dogs*", has owned two blind pugs and is an advocate for blind and visually impaired dogs.

Cathy resides in Massachusetts with her husband and their pug Digger.

For more information on blind dogs visit blind-devotion.com.

About the Illustrator

Anne Zimanski is a Michigan-based freelance artist. She has illustrated dozens of children's books and book covers, and works on a wide range of projects with clients from all over the world. Anne is also involved with local non-profit art groups, and loves to take part in teaching and spreading the love of art in her community.

To see more of Anne's work, visit annezimanski.com.

Follow Digger on Instagram!
@diggertheblindpug

Made in the USA
Lexington, KY
21 February 2018